A New Dawn

Compatible with

The 9th Age™

Impressum:

Written by the T9A Team

Published by FlorianGressConsulting, Rosenweg 24, 93053 Regensburg, Germany

Printed by Amazon Media EU S.à r.l., 5 Rue Plaetis, L-2338, Luxembourg

ISBN: 978-3-9824212-4-7

THE IX AGE
FANTASY BATTLES

A 9TH AGE SUPPLEMENT

SAURIAN ANCIENTS
A NEW DAWN

THE IX AGE
FANTASY BATTLES

A 9TH AGE SUPPLEMENT

SAURIAN ANCIENTS
A NEW DAWN

Faction leader: John Wallis

Head of Background: Edward Murdoch

Contributing authors: Andrew Barton, Edward Murdoch, Glenn Patel, Daniel Åkerman Sandberg, Alessandro Vivaldi, John Wallis, Calisson

Editor: John Wallis

Layout: Kacper Bucki

First Edition 09/2021

Saurians are the last great mystery of this world which once they ruled. Even today, the ruins of that pre-historic empire can be found in every corner of the globe, hinting at ancient technologies we can hardly begin to fathom. One such site still lurks within the copse at the western corner of my estate, and I go there sometimes to admire the jagged walls of smooth stone, so dark and polished it's almost like metal, even after so many millennia hidden under the vines and bushes that grow freely upon it.

Since their calamitous downfall, which we know only from myths, saurians have persisted in a much reduced state to torment and perplex the civilisations that have grown up in their absence. They confine themselves almost entirely to hidden enclaves throughout the hot parts of the world: desert, canyon, jungle, swamp or mountain are their homes, for despite their ferocious strength, they remain fearful of the mammalian species they once oppressed.

Some associate these reptilian bipeds with mysterious Virentia, perhaps owing to claims that the Dawn Age empire's great power was centred where the Shattered Sea now lies. But today there is no basis to this association: saurian populations are spread all over the world. Indeed, most scholars believe their greatest strength lies in the furthest east, in the undiscovered islands of the southern Sunrise Seas...

Many have sought but none have found the legendary realm of Atua, a magical island stronghold where no warm-blooded individual is permitted to set foot. Imagine it! The ancient glory of such a reptilian paradise! The saurians there communicate with their isolated kin in other enclaves through stepping portals, forming a global sorority of sorts – so some have claimed. But no such portal has ever been discovered, and if such an alliance exists, still it keeps to itself.

And yet from time to time, saurians do venture forth, and herein lies the greatest mystery. They do not seem to revel in war or bloodshed, and yet they regularly commit both. They are often builders or helpers – many are the accounts of desperate cities saved by the sudden arrival of cold-blooded labourers or miraculous shipments of food and supplies. Imperial officers have told me of battles that would have ended in massacres had not herds of gigantic reptilian monsters appeared, unasked for, to turn the tide. And yet there are just as many tales in which the saurians themselves are the monsters: cities razed, leaders and artefacts abducted, enemies supplied with fresh troops.

Considered as a whole, these strangest of peoples could plausibly be deemed mad, if not servants of random caprice and chaos. But I believe there must be another explanation. All the evidence I have found leads me to conclude that there has to be a method to the madness. That if we were only able to communicate, we could learn to understand why they behave the way they do. I am convinced that saurians have only the deepest respect for all life and for ordered civilisation. In fact, my hunch is that it is this very respect, carried to the point of fanaticism, that explains the saurians. Some alien and radical philosophy compels them to act in this method that seems so unpredictable and maddening to our eyes.

I am determined to get to the root of it, and now I believe I will have the chance. My good friend Wolfgang Hertzsche, by far the most accomplished man I know in the sadly under-developed field of saurian glyph translation, has made the necessary introductions for me in Zmayevatz, where happily it seems there are others who are equally convinced of the necessity of advancements in sauriology.

I have secured sponsorship for myself and my dear Natalya to conduct a preliminary expedition. The opportunity is thrilling, but the dangers are real. If I should fail to return, please ensure that my collection of saurian writings, assembled over decades of research, are forwarded directly to Herr Hertzsche. You will find them in the top drawer of my desk.

—Letter attached to the last will and testament of Milenko Petrovich, Knyaz of Smolnya

HISTORY

Covered with old, thick vines and moss, you couldn't tell it apart from your average rock. But while the dense greenery had made the small structure's once-proud surface unrecognizable, it had also done a marvelous job at protecting the interior from wind and rain.

As we cleared the opening, Ubalda Muric, the archeologist from Celeda Ablan, examined the stone that surrounded the eroded entryway, before turning to me with a thrill in his eyes. He lit a torch, reaching into the opening. The soft light revealed stairs leading down into the dark, remarkably intact. The crumbling entrance must have been raised at a later date; the interior was paved with stone and metal panels of a much finer quality, still smooth and glossy, reflecting the torchlight. It had been built by a more advanced but much older people. Probably in the Dawn Age itself.

The elf told his guards to wait outside while he and I entered, as they lacked archaeological training. My heart was pounding as I followed Ubalda down the stairs, into the realm of the Saurian Ancients.

I had been asked to join the archaeologist as a translator. I learned Arandad as a child, before I left my native Sagarika, and I have spent enough years now among both saurians and humans within the wide federation of Aotarakoan islands that spans much of this part of the ocean to have acquired something of both the warm-blood tongue and the cold-blood glyphs. I'd explored saurian ruins before, both on the islands and back on the subcontinent. The elves had been forced to acknowledge my usefulness, and break with their usual policy of dismissing human knowledge altogether.

As we arrived at the bottom, we were faced with a large, octagonal room. The geometric architecture of walls, floor and ceiling was flawless and astonishing. The surfaces were engraved with a complex series of precise lines and dots which I imagine may once have glowed with arcane lights. Even more striking were the mesmerizing images, painted in the distinct style of Golden Age saurian survivors. These images were entirely unrelated to the angular and alien patterns etched into the walls, and although very old, they were not as ancient as the walls themselves.

The pictures were beautiful, yet simplistic. Only a handful of colours were used, and most depicted landscapes of various kinds, some accompanied by a glyph or two.

Saurian... Future... Grim Tale... Remember or Listen... Perhaps a story. Perhaps a warning.

We saw stylised anurarchs, the legendary toadish tyrants, floating above a landscape of mountains, forests and lakes. Those closest to the earth operated huge, bizarre contraptions, or directed other saurians to build, to travel. The ones above them, however, were gazing towards the skies, complete with accurate constellations.

As the images continued, the stars became increasingly prominent. There were pictures of hands, reaching towards the heavens, as well as towards a bright, lone star I didn't recognise.

After this, there was an unsettling and drastic change. The images showed fires and dying saurians, the complex machinery smashed, the familiar landscapes ruined or flattened. In the center was a single, large glyph. I had not seen it before, but it looked like a combination of the words for "Invite" and "Death".

"Little is known about the Dawn Age," Ubalda told me, after I explained all this. "Even the best-kept records of Celeda Ablan are sparse, to say the least. But it would seem this is the very same story of the meteor sent by the gods to free us from saurian tyranny that was passed down by my ancestors. The rock struck the centre of their great machinery and cast it down, tearing the Veil, releasing daemons, forming a huge crater of poisoned sea."

The next images showed saurians fleeing, hiding away in mountains and concealed places. Some took to the sea – I recognised great *kaulua* canoe-rafts coming to these islands where we now stood. Finally, we saw an assortment of creatures, including saurians, massacring anurarchs with clubs and swords. Two runes at the bottom said simply: "Kill anurarchs".

Ubalda told me that anurarchs are in fact real creatures of vast and dangerous intellect, with an insatiable craving for knowledge and control, who are able to easily master every complex field, including magic. After the Dawn Age, they were thought to be extinct, only to reappear at the start of this age, after a great Inferno was unleashed by wicked dwarves in Augea.

"Centuries ago, we elves discovered increasing saurian activity, even across the oceans. Among other things, one of the founders of my university found these…"

Ubalda reached into his bag and retrieved a trio of stone tablets. I realised that his passion for archeology had overtaken his elven pride, forgetting that he was sharing precious findings with a human.

The tablets told of an armed conflict within the Atuan enclave. I had heard of the island of Atua from village elders on Aotarakoa. It was said to be a mysterious island somewhere in the middle of the vast oceans to the east, that only the saurians could find. A holy island in which their kind first came together and formed the philosophy of the *koru* spiral (which most call "Vitalism"), to preserve and spread life. The conflict described on these stone tablets seemed to center around the re-emergence of the anurarchs. While some saurians saw great potential to use these creatures' powers on behalf of Vitalism, there were others who wanted the anurarchs dead on sight, believing they were inherently tyrannical and would once again try to enslave the world.

Ubalda ran his finger across the text as he continued, as if reading to a child.

"At the end of the civil war, a compromise was reached. The anurarchs would be protected as advisors and mages, but they would be closely guarded and kept separate from society. Under their guidance and magical support, envoys of the Atuan enclave began traveling. Our Royal Navy encountered many large, saurian ships never before seen. Most of them were destroyed, of course, but how many more reached their destinations? It was as if, suddenly, something that had been asleep for ages awoke within saurian minds. They started meeting, cooperating and building. But most of all, they made alliances, forming a global network called simply, the Collaboration."

He sighed. "Alas, there's still much we don't understand. Come. Let us get some fresh air. I cannot think properly in this damp place."

—*Memoirs of Indira Padhi, former traveller of the Sunrise Seas.*

VITALISM
Vitalism and You

Do you find the world around you confusing and troubling? Do jealousy and greed disturb your petty dreams? Are you left unsatisfied by the race for personal gain?

Our morality, Vitalism, offers the correct outlook upon the world you know, and a new place you must fulfil within it.

All life follows a natural pattern. Growth, reproduction and decay. This last, the decline and deterioration of all things: this is the great enemy, whose name is entropy. Over time, mighty temples erode to dust. The hottest furnaces cool and darken. A drop of ink in a large pool disperses to nothing. The cosmos itself fades and intermingles until any meaning is lost. Only through the preservation and growth of life itself, the miracle of self-replication, can this entropy be held at bay.

The best and self-evident way, our way, is to act as custodians: to weed out threats in our gardens, and encourage new growth. This work compels us at all stages of our existence. From birth, we know the value of life: never take more than necessary, never destroy wantonly, only use violence to further the needs of Vitalism.

Simply put, our lives – and now yours – must bring more value and discrete information into the world than we are responsible for taking out.

To this end, you must avoid destructive actions and technologies. We do not destroy living things to acquire surplus resources. We do not begin fires, which consume and reduce information into ash. We are not wasteful; nothing that can be put to productive purpose is discarded.

This is also in our minds and morals. Unlike your people, we do not lie, as falsehoods can only lead to decay. Ownership and theft are not part of our world: resources are allocated by need, not by desire. We do not hold to lost causes – life is worth more than imaginary concepts like your "honour", which have no existence in the world. We do not follow gods, who seek only their own power. We never allow chaos to take hold, to break the ties that bind us together. All life should recognise the importance of Vitalism and collaborate to improve the universe.

In time, you will see the wisdom of the self-evident way. You must acknowledge our greater understanding and unity of purpose. We can still allow differences – pure uniformity is as destructive and non-discrete as chaos. Only change allows growth. Even the right art reflects this – an unchanging pattern only symbolises the horror of the infinite. Instead, by creating complex patterns which never repeat, we represent the purest means of undoing entropy. We will teach you the differences which are positive, and which are wasteful and unnecessary.

Some will claim we seek to enslave the world, as in stories of the Dawn Age. We fear such stories as much as you. If our ancestors really behaved in such a way, their conflicts and attempts to control only harmed the world, and ended in catastrophe. We wish simply to bring aid and alliance to the unenlightened. Our battles cause us great grief. But we are prepared to defend our mission and to protect life itself, to ensure our message can survive until it takes root.

Do you see the truth? Do you recognise that Vitalism is superior to squabbling over material gains or temporary power? Now you must learn from us, and serve the future as we do.

This message was delivered by saurian emissaries to the court of the Great Khan Jirandai, seeking to persuade our people to abandon gunpowder and cookfires. The Great Khan entertained them, as with all visitors, though their arrogance and presumption angered many.

Realising their unintended insult, the saurians later returned with a more gentle and less condescending version of the pamphlet, written in slightly better Gyenggetat. Seeking to persuade, rather than cajole, it invited us to "work together towards a shared goal". This attempt at diplomacy proved counter-productive; ogres respect strength of conviction even if the words offended.

Saurians may not have gods, but they clearly believed in their mission with a religious zeal. The ogres called them humourless and lifeless, but I confess I found their concern with an epic cosmic battle of which none of us are even aware quite exciting. Their deeply emotional conception of life-as-miracle is undeniably endearing. Alas, I fear I enjoy my campfires too much to fully subscribe to the Vitalist calling just yet! – PC

*—Found among the correspondence between Pascaline Caillat,
the woman "raised by ogres", and Hélène de Montprat*

THE COLLABORATION

Listen to me! Listen to the words that travel the skies and seas!

The spiral must ever grow! Choose life; choose life, for death is eager to choose you!

The spiral has ever grown, and I have followed in its wake!

Death is upon us; aye, death is all around. Death is in fire, death is in spears, death lurks forever, and only new life can push it away. We are all the makers of the spiral, and I am the speaker!

Learn now of the growth of the spiral! Learn now of the great work! Learn now!

The ground from which the spiral grows is sacred! It is the home of the storm! From the skies come water, from water comes life, and from the eye of the storm comes wisdom!

It is a new growth, a new life! The spiral grows in the hearts of those who once, aye, may have been enemies, but no longer! The people of the storm had hope that life could be reborn! They had hope that ancient days could be ash, and from the ash could grow the spiral!

Life finds a way! The spiral grows!

It began in the storm, but it grew! The spiral grew to my home! To the islands of my people, to Aotarakoa! *Tangatapunga*, the lizard people, became *tangatakoru*, the people of the spiral, and the *tangatakoru* became our friends! The spiral grew in their hearts!

The spiral grew beyond the islands of the sky and storm! It grew to the islands of fire! It grew in the heart and it grew by the sea, carried in mighty boats of old! The spiral grew in purpose! The spiral is life itself, and without the spiral, life is nothing but ash to be!

So the words were carried to Patareng, to those who live in the shadow of the dragons! Life pits itself against fire, and fire shall not win! Aye, I have seen your dragons, I have seen the people, I speak my words to you! The spiral grows!

The islands of fire were not the end of the spiral! The spiral grows!

The spiral grew, from storm to sky to fire to earth! Far from this place is the land in which things grow! Life grew to life! The spiral proved itself, a circle complete! In Oaxtepetl, life grows beyond the bounds of the mind! I have seen the nearest shores, seen the beasts that shake the ground with a tread!

Aye, I have travelled! I have followed the path of the spiral! I have followed it across the world and back again! I have seen wonders, and I have seen the emptiness between the lines of the spiral! The spiral ever grows, but the spiral is not all that is!

I have followed the path of the spiral to the lands of shadow, death and dread! The spiral grows, and it has grown into the heart of darkness! It has grown into the land of the sunset! The spiral has grown to the *tangatapunga* of the land of ten thousand cattle! I have seen the herds that move like insects upon the ground, so great are their numbers! The spiral grows!

The spiral grows in the heart. Cast aside the eaters of ash! Cast aside the spirits born of chaos and death! Cast aside your parasite gods! Life is the only cause worthy of life! The spiral grows!

1/3

I heard this speech during my brief stay at the court of Yongxin, a small province on the coast, spoken by envoys from the uncivilised islands of the distant south. It seems these people have long been in league with saurians, not understanding them as lesser descendents of the Dawn Ancestors as we do, though their saurians are a different tribe to those that dwell in the hotter regions of our own nation.

Most of the court dismissed the islanders as raving barbarians, but the speaker's words intrigued me. When I returned to Longjing, I requested some time for personal study and investigated several Halls of Records.

I have confirmed my intuition that the spread of the "spiral" symbolises the creation of what other reptilians have called the Collaboration. According to the most venerable archivists, this is a poorly-understood global network that emerged during the last thousand years, when the saurians set sail on mighty rafts to find their kin in other enclaves. Some say that these missions succeeded in re-activating sites left dormant since the Dawn Age, sites which facilitate magical, instantaneous travel between distant lands. Their goal was seemingly to unite the isolated tribes under a moral crusade that our scholars catalogue by the name Vitalism, a minor heresy.

I believe that the islander's spiral is the metaphor for Vitalism. It begins at "the home of the storm", which is surely the fearful Atua, an uncharted land said to lie in the midst of an unnavigable ocean. It must be from here the rafts departed.

It spreads to the islander's home, where her people are converted – though they were likely not the Atuans' intended targets, but rather the native saurians who lived alongside. I found only one helpful document, which describes Aotarakoa as a volcanic realm, where the so-called *tangatakoru* exploit the earth's heat using long cables of swordgrass. It seems that the name Aotarakoa has since spread to other islands of the region, forming its own confederation of indigenous humans.

Next is Patareng, called the "islands of fire" apparently as a reference to the influence of the Dragon Emperor. It's true we maintain small but active trade routes with these comparatively nearby islands, which are a valuable source of jade among other commodities. Some sailors claim to have seen vast, ornate temples within the jungle built entirely of that precious stone – the effect is said to be exceptionally beautiful and harmonious. Here, the saurians are thought to practice unique forms of meditation which grant their warriors extraordinary, weaponless fighting skills, and their toad-mages the ability to project their souls beyond their bodies to wander the Mortal and Immortal realms alike. Such implausible tales even extend to supernals visiting the reptiles in return! In any case, Patareng's Vitalism is surely tempered significantly by such a mystical native culture.

After Patareng, the references are harder to track. I did eventually find a file on Oaxtepetl, a Virentian enclave hidden in deep valleys behind elaborate traps – it's thought to be the source of the Collaboration's
extraordinary access to giant monsters, as mentioned in the speech. My research suggests the saurians
of that land already had a healthy respect for nature, which must have made them easy converts to Vitalism. There is some suggestion that they have made treaties with the local humans who build great pyra-
mids and make live sacrifices to their gods, though such bloodthirsty savages seem highly incompatible
with Vitalist philosophy.

We know that there are dozens of enclaves within the Collaboration, but the last one mentioned by the
Aotarakoan was "the land of ten thousand cattle". Its location near to the "lands of dread" suggests this
is a Silexian enclave, and indeed after many days of searching I did find a sole mention of "Wanahtas", a
series of deep canyons in the arid heartland of the continent. Here, the reptiles compete with beast herds
over domestic livestock. If my reading is correct, they even ride horses, and enforce their principles with
considerably more enthusiasm and violence than other Collaborators, if the report is to be believed.

The fascinating diversity of the enclaves presented by the islanders leads me to conclude that a longer
report is warranted, including a serious attempt to catalogue a full list of Collaboration members.

—*Copy of report by Tsuandanese administrator Shi Gengxin*

BIOLOGY

Milenko still thinks there must be a pattern: some kind of guiding reason that explains the ancient reptiles' unfathomable behaviour, offering aid with one hand and war with the other. He's been speaking to that buffoon Wolfgang again, with his glyphs that supposedly reveal some kind of cosmic battle between life and decay.

In any event, Milenko is all fired up about the expedition. I've tried explaining that I prefer to study my specimens in the privacy of our own home, but he insists that the true naturalist must observe her subjects in the wild. I can hardly disagree with that... and I suppose he is my husband.

We set sail in August.

After trekking through an arid savannah devoid of civilisation, we are now encamped in outright desert. It's a damnable, craggy land, with strange formations of stone and salt, the very dirt hot to the touch and hissing with foul vapours.

It took days of searching – several times we followed signs that I believe were intentionally left as misdirection. Finally, by chance I noticed some artificial earthworks by a dried-up riverbed – the stream had been diverted, and by following its cunningly hidden course, we were able to find it: the saurian city of Kitwana. It was completely obscured from the view of any who were not looking for it, deep inside a canyon between two impenetrable mesa formations, carved from natural caves with almost invisible openings in the cliffs. Even after days of searching, we would never have found it, had we not been fortunate to spy a group of reptilians darting through the entrance without seeing us.

Tomorrow we will attempt to get a better look.

Milenko is frustrated. After months of observing Kitwana from our camp atop the mesa, he is no closer to understanding their nature. But for my own part, I have found these last weeks more fruitful than I ever thought possible. This truly is the most fascinating of the intelligent species.

And it's not even a coherent entity. I can now confirm Misernach's theory that the saurian people consist of four separate castes: highly divergent branches of a single mono-reproductive species, in that each is able to lay eggs hatching the others. I can't say how such an unusual arrangement arose – the possibility of intentional specio-genesis by ancient magics cannot be discounted, though there's no good evidence for it either.

I will use the names commonly applied in the literature: *skinks* are the smallest, nimblest and, I believe, the shortest lived. While they rarely exceed more than four feet in height, their scale-armoured cousins the *tegus* often grow to a full seven. These individuals are somewhat more deliberate and sturdy, though they share most tasks with the skinks and clearly possess a near-identical intellect.

Together, these two castes account for ninety percent of the saurian population of Kitwana. The remainder is composed largely of *caimans*: encrusted, eight-foot monsters of great strength, whose temperament is normally most otherworldly and ponderous, though they are extremely frightening when roused. I witnessed one ferociously seeing off an enraged wild karkadan that had strayed too close to the enclave. They are longer lived, I suspect, behaving like wisened elders, protectors of tradition, teachers of philosophy and warfare alike. While the caimans aid in communal work, they mostly spend free time in isolated meditation and queer artistic pursuits, carving intricate glyphs or tending delicate flowers and miniature trees...as well as honing a range of vicious and unsettling weaponry.

Artistry is by no means unique to caimans – skinks and tegus spend hours upon hours carving inexplicable patterns and alien statues. The valley is littered with their decorated monoliths, some of the smaller ones floating eerily above the earth, or pulsing with coloured lights – impressive feats of construction considering they do not build any structures for shelter or work.

Only the fourth kind of saurian shows little interest in such labours: the *anurarchs*, a name of most ancient and terrible foreboding, thought until quite recently to be entirely mythical or long extinct. This unique caste is, I believe, reptilian like its kin, but it gives the appearance of a bloated amphibian, several feet in diameter, its limbs atrophied, spending its long life almost entirely motionless. In all of Kitwana I have seen only two anurarchs, and they are kept separate, tended by the other saurians and guarded at all times by gangs of tegu warriors.

Naturally, these four species are not the only creatures that inhabit the hidden city. There are also the larger reptiles, the "Magna Sauria", which lack intelligence and are used like beasts of burden – and sometimes, I believe, kept purely for companionship. The variety and forms of these massive beasts are stunning – more so when you consider that such species are not found in the wild anywhere on the continent. Then there are the livestock, both avian and mammalian, kept in pens and pastures and used exclusively for meat.

All saurians are carnivorous, and I believe they are also ecto-thermic, being sluggish in the morning shade, and vigorous in the heat of the day. They display considerable diversity of colouration – most are brown or sand-coloured, but some groups have yellow and even red or black patterning. None are anything like the bright blue and violet Augean specimens I studied in Narrenwald. The most exotic are those which can adapt their colours to their surroundings, blending so cleverly with the landscape that they can only be seen when moving.

They have returned my journal, but my fate remains uncertain. It has been four months, I think, since they killed my fool of a husband after he tried to capture and interrogate their skink scouts. My grief and fury has passed. I am already learning to communicate – neither they nor I can make the sounds necessary to speak the other's language, but we are developing a series of gestures for basic concepts, and we are studying each other's writing.

I must admit that this time I have spent in the heart of Kitwana has been by far the most stimulating of my life. I understand I am a prisoner here, but I have also realised that I would not wish to leave. I am beginning to get to know individual saurians beyond the mere Vitalist principles they use for names. Far from the emotionless automatons that are described on the battlefield, these people have personalities and deep feelings. They bond with one another, can experience loneliness, and greatly mourn all forms of death.

It's true that their facial musculature does not allow for the same breadth of expression as humans – it looks impassive and alien to our eyes. Equally, I am certain that my mentor Sonya Kuragin was correct when she argued that the saurian auricular organ is receptive to a wider range of sounds than our own – they can thereby transfer simple stimuli and emotions over long distances without any need for direct mental contact. I believe this creates a *de facto* communal sentience among the population, allowing it to sense danger or operate in tandem, for example, in ways that most mammals cannot – accounting for battlefield reports of eerie synchronicity.

Next month will be the ten-year anniversary of my arrival at Kitwana. I regret having neglected this journal of late, but I feel little need to record my observations in my old, human fashion, just as I no longer feel the need to pray to old gods. Still, writing is a wonderful source of discrete and lasting information: the anti-entropic principle that we must all pursue to improve the universe.

Today I witnessed the miracle of the start of hatching season, which is always a humbling honour. The males hatch first, their tiny eggs kept in bowls of warm desert soil, from which they scurry loose, initially no bigger than my thumb. Saurians demonstrate extreme dimorphism – these males exist only to perpetuate the epic wonder of life itself, never gaining intelligence or growing larger than a common gecko, running free until it is time to fertilise new eggs. Soon will come the larger eggs of the true saurians, the females, whose awesome task it is to safeguard the future of the cosmos itself. There is an egg this year, more spherical than the others, which some think will prove to be an anurarch. It seems there is no way to know until they hatch – while mothers of one caste can produce any of the others, none can control the proportions of each type within a clutch of eggs. The old naturalist in me finds this fascinating.

I can't wait to see the younglings, so full of life and hope! I believe saurians are able to pass memories to their offspring, or at least highly-developed instincts, for when they emerge they seem already to know the skills their parents possess. They can forage, fight and negotiate the treacherous landscape from their first day of life. If only we unenlightened mammals were so well evolved.

—Extracts from the diary of Natalya Petrovich, herpetologist and former Knyaginya of Smolnya,
supplied to a merchant caravan by saurian missionaries in northern Taphria

GOVERNMENT

When I was passing through Zmayevatz one snowy November, it so happened that I had the opportunity to recite at a certain tavern in the university district. My tale that night proved popular with the house, but I was still surprised by the generous tip that was forwarded to me afterwards by a well-dressed, hirsute gentleman dining alone in the corner. I approached him, feeling obliged to offer my thanks.

"A fine tale is a rare gift," he replied, and gestured at the seat opposite him. "Join me, and perhaps I can provide one in return."

I accepted the offer, and learned that I was in the company of one W. Hertzsche, an ambassador and a linguist almost as gifted as my own humble self. But his real passion was the deciphering of –

"Saurian glyphs," I exclaimed, seeing the notebook he had open before him.

"You recognise them?" he asked, raising an eyebrow.

"You see, I once encountered –" I began, but he ignored me, looking down at the drawings in his book.

"These symbols were found on documents seized by the dwarves of Nevaz Derom when they annihilated a saurian enclave ten years ago. The dwarven attack was provoked by a saurian act of sabotage, which had carefully melted the hold's entire arsenal of cannons for no clear reason. Perhaps you would like to know what the documents say."

I nodded solemnly, recognising a rare moment when it was better to stay silent than to keep talking. I quickly extracted my own notebook so I could record his words, while all around us the firelit tavern bustled.

"I believe they are government files," Herr Hertzsche began. "But not a government in a sense that we would recognise. As far as I can tell, each saurian enclave organises itself in its own unique way, but very few have any kind of hierarchy or rulers, just as they follow no gods. Our instinctive desire for power seems entirely foreign to their reptilian minds. Individuals within an enclave take it in turns to act as simple administrators, rather than leaders or policy-makers. Even on the battlefield, they show little interest in human concepts of honour, loyalty or duty to carry out orders or obey authorities. They have never been observed to seek personal prestige or glory. When major decisions must be made, the enclave meets to discuss the matter and find a consensus on how to proceed – always gravitating towards compromise. This text records the events at one such meeting. You are welcome to read it yourself."

He turned the page to reveal his translation in neat lines of Sonnstahlisch. His eyes flickered in the candlelight, and I almost shuddered. To this day, I'm not sure why he showed me his work. Perhaps he just wanted not to be the only one who had read the words of a dead, cold-blooded tribe who we may never understand.

As the barmaid called last orders, I read the following words:

It is time to discuss the Self-Evident Imperative to increase lasting
information in the world. We should not be content with improving
only ourselves and our kind. We can do more good if other peoples join us.

> We have discussed this matter before. Unenlightened peoples can destroy
> information and life when we try to communicate with them. We do not know
> their minds, as they do not know ours. They are unpredictable, the risk is too high.

We have not discussed it for a long time. Some unenlightened are less
destructive than others. They can be taught. The small ones,
the hairy-faces. They work with stone. They make lasting objects.
They create writing, they store information, prevent degradation.
They do good works for the universe. They could be Collaborators.

> Those hair-skinks use great fire. They protect deep enclaves.
> They hate other people. They are not Collaborators.

We should talk to hair-skinks and bring them information about Cosmological
Morality. Then they will not use great fire. They will not hate other people.

> The hairy-axes will not understand Cosmological Morality.
> They will say it is not right, just like other unenlightened people.

The Self-Evident Imperative of Cosmological Morality demands that living people
should work together to improve the universe, not separately. It is known.

> The Self-Evident Imperative of Cosmological Morality implies that
> living people should not kill each other. If unenlightened people
> see Enlightened People, living people will kill each other.
> They hate Enlightened People because of differences.
> They hate Enlightened People because of old stories.

*Discourse continued for thirty-nine segments. One hundred seventy-one vocal contributors. Two primary
viewpoints identified. Consensus reached on the following compromise-solution:*

Stealthy removal of small-mammals' great fire instruments. Then they will be Collaborators.

Seasonal administrators will organise operations for execution of compromise-solution.

> *—Copied among the writings of Samuel le Pepin, professional pilgrim and storyteller*

RELATIONSHIPS

You wish to know of the scaled ancients, those who were here long before the first raft reached any island? The *tangatakoru?*

We do not speak clearly to them, nor they to us. I think they cannot. Their mouths are not like ours, and so their voices are not like ours. Still, we know some things.

They are guides, guardians, judges, avengers: avatars of water and stone. You want to know why they have not destroyed us? Listen, then, of our beginnings.

Long ago, before we built our houses and our docks and our fortifications, this island was a place for fishermen to visit. The harbour is bounteous, and shielded from storms, so some decided to stay, to build a new home. They made a little village, and in the night, a line of fresh-planted seedlings with red leaves appeared, not far into the bush. "This far, and no further," was the message.

This was fine; we were fishermen, we did not need the land.

When the raiders came, they made a mistake: they crossed the line trying to ambush us. They were dead before their fifth pace.

We knew who had made the line, for we had seen them – our saviours, intended or not. Green and blue, scaled like the little lizards who sunned themselves on warm rocks.

They watched us from the land, and we watched them from the edge of the sea.

Then came their emissary, a tiny little thing, like a child. She drew pictures on the sand: first the *koru*, the unfolding spiral of the fern. We called her Koru at first, after that symbol, for she pointed at herself, but it was not so. Her people were the people of the Koru, believers in life, and growth. So we named them, in time. They wish for all things to grow and be blessed – the fish, the pigs, the trees, the ferns, even humans.

They are not warlike; they do not wish to die, nor do they wish to kill.

So I ask you, pale man – what have you done to make them destroyers?

— Transcription of the words of Kaikauwhata of Aotarakoa

ANURARCHS

Quick Hope Increase, dear you,

The hope is there that the communication is found to you in good and amenable ways. The importance of the subject to which I about speak is high and I take interest in your opinion and thought.

Many are saying that anurarchs to our society bring much, but I am sure not at all. Certainly they intelligent are, but scheming they may also be. Others my concern share and question whether anurarch advice and counsel taken should be. There is worry that they are curious overly and inquisitive beyond measure. I am fearful that they may work against us and look for opinion as to combat this how.

The enclave continues a search local for tablets lost. Tablets of a nature highly useful. The administrators chose specifically to include not any anurarch in their plannings, but ago two nights, I found Anurarch Togetherness in her designated zone with unauthorised maps of sites possible of tablet thieves.

Confronted her did I, questioning why she had them and replied with an arrogance did she that I expected not. Stated did she that her reasons were her own and that curiosity of an enclave's plans was not a cause for concern. She informed to me that enlightenment comes from questions. That questions new knowledge may give, and that anti-entropic goals may achieved be by seeking advice from one such as she.

What you suggest, do I?

Regards of warmth,
Ever Warm Coherence

Ever Warm Coherence, dear you,

To hear of you is joyous and your words of salutation I do welcome. Your concerns I understand and such discussions have taken place here, to tell of truth.

But I am to say that your mistrusting is misplaced and merit it does not warrant. Proven have the anurarchs been. Their support of Vitalism is most favourable; healing, construction and war they much help provide to; advice from them is sought by my enclave regularly. The past should not be forgotten, but does it dictate the future neither. Put aside your suspicions, look anew to the teachings between one another, and only then will 'us' and 'them' become 'we'.

Regards of warmth,
Quick Hope Increase

Quick Hope Increase, dear you,

Your words are kind and your advice welcome do I. But of this I am sure still not. No doubt have I, in all enclaves an anurarch is given tegu guards – some protectors say, others jailors. Of late, however, Anurarch All-Growth sighted was, bodyguard without, around the grounds of night late.

Guards at post believed they were, within sights the anurarch. Somehow tricked they were; my friend Most Enlightening Energy saw Anurarch All-Growth in the western caves unaccompanied. She to unseen person spoke, then she this someone incinerated with magefire, oh most evil! Deny the attack she did not. The burned stranger an assassin was, she claimed: she merely against an attacker defended herself, who had abducted her from her guards.

Dangerous is it not, to freedom give them? For the more we may give, the more they invariably take. Their intelligence desirable but also most fearful is, and I believe to ignore this at our peril we may do so. Can you say honestly, what be their ultimate goal? Their strategies complex can be, they can see long of term and their teachings may in fact be of a plan we can not yet see. I do not think it so unlikely is that anurarchs intend for final power and returned tyranny, as many good Vitalists claim. If that true be, they intend must surely to confidence gain and warm-blood loyalty create among we the Enlightened.

Regards of warmth,
Ever Warm Coherence

Ever Warm Coherence, dear you,

And what if your anurarch used fire in western caves? The anurarch defended herself. Ash and death regrettable are, but the greater good outweighs unfortunate consequences.

Only one anurarch in my enclave there is, and regard and respect greatest she has. Of her teachings and deeds the good is wide and shared by our society and our administrators. Just two moons previous I almost killed was by falling monolith while carving self-evident patterns. Several tall stones collapse did but was lost no life. Our anurarch used unknown spells to me and others save. I watched her restore monoliths their places to with no anti-entropic information harmed.

I do not believe that harm they wish for us. I believe that they wish universe good fortune and positive intent, because self-evident truth they have learned. We may not yet know fully what they plan, but I, and my enclave, do not ignorance allow to fear create – as in days long ago of Great Evil Strife.

These times are fractious and delicate, implore you do I to with your administrators speak and look to collaborate with your anurarch rather than against her work.

May the stars favourably shine on you and our world.

Regards of warmth,
Quick Hope Increase

—Missives between the Talbaatar and Montecorto enclaves.
Translator has attempted to retain the syntax of the original glyphs.

I have been spending time with Anurarch Nurturing. Unlike Anurarch Vital, she is quite communicative, able to form the basic sounds required for speech with other saurians (to me they seem little more than clicks and hissing). Since, unlike other saurians, anurarchs have lips, she was also able to approximate Volskayan after I had spoken with her for a few hours.

I asked her about Anurarch Vital's preference for speaking directly into my mind. She was happy to explain – it seems many anurarchs practice a form of spellcraft that connects their thoughts with others over a certain distance. Some, like Anurarch Vital, therefore disdain physical speech, and communicate almost entirely by magic; in extreme cases such cerebral stimulation can even become an addictive craving. Other anurarchs apparently have no interest in these games, dedicating their magical studies towards other paths, perfectly content to speak out loud like the rest of us. Anurarchs are creatures of study and learning, consumed by curiosity and interest in many fields. While they have no innate magical abilities, they surpass the archmages of Sonnstahl in mastery of the arcane, thanks purely to their own self-teaching.

Even among those who do employ mental contact, it seems there is a considerable variety in technique and ability. Some can merely sense emotions or project brief images rather than fully formed words. Some can only hear their conversational partner, others can only speak to them. Most can communicate in languages they already know, but a few are able to translate directly into a tongue spoken by the listener. The most advanced, dedicated anurarchs have apparently been able to read the thoughts and memories of another without their conscious communication. Rarer still is the ability to nudge or even control the target's mind, making them an unwilling puppet, but Anurarch Nurturing would not tell me more about this or the other exotic forms of this strange spell.

—Extract from the diary of Natalya Petrovich, delivered to colonists in southern Taphria

TECHNOLOGY

§1, The souls of metals.

Most smiths lack the subtlety to understand the process I have demonstrated theoretically, to change the soul of a metal into the soul of another metal. I was intrigued to hear about the sudden influx of gold coming from our trading posts in Taphria. Perhaps someone has completed the transmutation process! Here is a chance to find the true Philosopher's Stone and prove my detractors wrong. Prince Rudolf II von Kölen was kind enough to loan me the resources to bring back the Stone. Blessed be his benevolent love for science.

§6, Meeting a legend.

I was directed to the famous Doctor Eric Tombstone (as I presumed I would be), in a Vanhu village near Josepha Falls. He knew of a nearby community of saurians using esoteric technology which fitted the description. He found a guide and interpreter, Jina, who speaks our tongue and understands saurian body language and some of their glyphs.

§8, Meeting native saurians.

The reptiles hide themselves from other species in a concealed settlement the Vanhu call Motomjusi. It lies somewhere across a gigantic lake by a smoking volcano surrounded by dense woods. The saurians found us as we approached; we were blindfolded and taken by dark, winding paths to a huge bipedal saurian, a caiman, living in a former lava tunnel – a mere outpost of the main enclave. Jina understood from various gestures that her "name" was "Discretely Preserved", and told me she knew many technological secrets, although to me she looked more like a shaman. She had carved and painted her tunnel with various glyphs in ultra-complex, irregular patterns. Perhaps some form of magnum opus?

§9, Absence of modern technology.

I was initially unimpressed. No forge, workshop, powder keg or arsenal exist among the saurians. They can make neither glass nor ploughs. Lacking steel, saurians use sharp obsidian blades to cut. Their knowledge of metal is primitive, barely enough for bronze, which they use sparingly.

They despise fire like a sin. They draw heat from the earth itself, using mechanisms I don't recognise. They warm dense basalt stones against the lava tunnels of the volcano itself, to accumulate the heat and keep it stored.

§10, Sauria Mundi, an alleged worldwide guild.

When I asked Discretely Preserved about her large collection of seashells, surprising so far from the ocean, she explained that her community was not isolated, but part of a wider guild, which shares its discoveries. She pretended it extended across the world – a laughable claim for natives who rarely leave their village. They dream that they can travel across continents, using gates which open here on one side, elsewhere on the other side. They feign to have shared many discoveries through that network. This is unbelievable. Nevertheless, they do have unexplained ways to communicate; I have witnessed their disturbing ability to transfer emotions between non-proximate individuals. Discretely Preserved occasionally stiffens at something only she can sense.

§11, Astronomy.

When the caiman finally believed my intentions were purely scientific, I was at last permitted to enter the enclave proper – though I was once again blindfolded on the way.

It is truly a wonder to behold, swarming with productive labourers of different sizes, with many species of Magna Sauria roaming freely among them, and everything illuminated by ubiquitous and colourful artwork. There is nothing like it in any civilisation of our species, I am quite certain. I will attempt to describe the astonishing sights individually, but in truth their combined effect was greater than the sum of its parts – I confess that my knees nearly gave way more than once in those first few hours.

There are many mysteries in this saurian community. Despite having no lord, priest or inquisitor, they seem to be organized seamlessly and can complete complex tasks together, with little verbal discussion. They repair any broken or degraded thing with utmost urgency, as if their lives depend on it. They have few buildings, but their architecture is brilliant in its oddity.

Among the many strange monoliths, which I assume are purely artistic, loom different kinds of towers, sixty feet high and made of polished bricks fit together with extreme precision without mortar. They are decorated with bright and interlacing stones. Their main purpose is allegedly to capture and collect heat – in this instance, from the very aether. It makes no sense, but I believe it has to do with the large crystal lenses and obsidian mirrors focusing the sun's light. The towers are thus heated to blistering temperatures, and a series of conductive metals channel this heat to cooler parts of the enclave – those underground, or in the shade – keeping them warm even into the night. There are also stations where an individual saurian can remove a slab of treated basalt, pack it in special insulators of their own design, and wear it on their back as a portable source of heat for long journeys.

Yet other kinds of towers are said to be placed at angles and distances linked with astronomy. I thought it was a metaphor, but Discretely Preserved predicted a solar eclipse to the very hour, using a complex stellar observation device reflecting lights on curved mirrors coupled with delicate bronze gearings. I suspect she used magic formulas to help.

§12, Magnetism.

The first time I saw a saurian levitating, I recognized a more powerful version of the magnetic phenomenon the alchemists of Santa Regina produce by wiping straws with amber. Saurians use natural lodestone instead, though later I discovered that magic is used regularly to enhance the magnetic potency. Still, it is extraordinary to witness iron attracted by one magnetite stone and repelled by another. This is the scientific proof that stones and iron have souls!

Discretely Preserved noticed my enthusiasm and showed me various tools using magnetism. I had to leave all the steel I was carrying, in fear of being stuck or injured. This is probably why they don't use such materials in their weapons.

Levitation is fascinating. It can lift heavy charges and keep them stable over rough terrain, removing any need for paved roads. The lack of friction makes moving heavy weights effortless. Simple spells are used to "charge" the ground, so it repels the lodestones.

A skink called "Immutable Nine", who for some reason had a piece of eggshell on her head, invited me to hurl my paring knife at her. Despite what I thought was quite a strong throw, she deflected the object several feet before it reached her, simply using a small spear I had assumed to be quite primitive.

§13, Crystal and the search for the Philosopher's Stone.

Saurians know many distinct stones and crystals besides obsidian and magnetite. They use green peridot and other blue, yellowish or red crystals which I could not identify. These provide glowing lights in darkness, creating colourful patterns throughout the enclave and again avoiding the need for flames at night. Each of the stones seems to talk to the soul of a different metal! A black crystal from the volcano, more granular than obsidian, influences iron magnetite, heating it while levitating.

Now it is clear: since metal souls interact with the souls of precious stones, they must be somehow related. I have to reconsider my works from the start to incorporate these fascinating discoveries.

§15. Research required.

With the limited tools at hand, I cannot experiment as I wish. I trust Jina to bring these words to Dr. Tombstone, who I kindly ask to forward them to the university, along with a request to send me urgently: 1 furnace, 2 crucibles…

—Excerpts of notes assembled for an unpublished work,
"On the Transmutation of the Soul of Metals", by Ramon-Arnau Llulls de Vilanova

MAGNA SAURIA

As it has many times before, the *Poodle* has delivered us safely to our destination. Aguadulce has not much to recommend it, but we will be heading inland soon. I am excited at a chance to encounter the many kinds of giant reptiles that others have found in this land, and which exist nowhere else in the world except among saurian enclaves. Even in Virentia, their only native realm, they have proven hard to find for many expeditions, but I am confident we are sufficiently equipped to succeed.

It is well documented that the Magna Sauria are extensively domesticated by their smaller, sapient cousins for military, economic and possibly ecological purposes. Presumably by using the mysterious magics with which the Dawn Age coldbloods somehow cross the world, the beasts seem to have been distributed among the many enclaves that are known to collaborate worldwide. But what is less understood is how these spectacular species live, breed, and feed in the wild when they are free of the saurians' domesticating influence.

Day 3

I've traveled extensively through Vetia, Augea and Taphria, but Virentia is proving even more sublime in its wealth of flora and fauna. The creatures here are both beautiful and terrible, though their marvels are lost on my companions, I fear. Our party is three hundred strong – mostly Destrian military, with a few native guides.

Day 15

We finally reached the Lagarto river. In twelve days, we lost fifteen men on the savannah. I've helped the officers deal with big cats, pythons and crocodiles, but none of us had previous experience with raptors. These are the only species of Magna Sauria which can be found in the wild outside of Virentia, and certain scholars have published extensively on their varied taxonomy. Some veterans have seen them in battle, ridden by both saurians and elves, but none could anticipate their behavior in a natural state. Like other apex predators, they hunt in packs, exceptionally stubborn and coordinated, even able to plan ambushes. One pack followed us for almost two days, waiting for the right moment to attack isolated groups – swift and rarely seen.

The raptor genus shows greater diversity than previously known: I had the chance to observe species of various shapes, colours and sizes. Notably, some display long feathers in the savannah, while those living closer to the Lagarto exhibit brown or green hides to blend in with the denser foliage. One frilled species was even seen to project an exotic, corrosive saliva to deter competitors and larger predators.

Day 26

The land is as dangerous as it is wonderful. We've now passed the southern tributary of the Lagarto, leaving the swamps for deep jungle. 56 men are dead. Everyone is afraid. It seems they do not understand the sacrifices we must make for great discoveries.

My subjects are as huge and terrifying as they are fascinating. I should have been careful what I wished for. Even the herbivores can kill you without meaning to. Yesterday we lost four men to a herd of frenzied, fleeing creatures similar to Taphrian ostriches, but three yards tall. These were the largest examples of what I have dubbed the *Struthiosaur* genus – the most common reptilians so far encountered, which the natives call *tlaltototl*, ground birds.

Day 29

After the herd had passed, we lost another dozen men in the worst attack yet: carnosaurs. I had heard of these monsters but could not believe their enormity and ferociousness. If they had not been pursuing the struthiosaurs, our casualties would have been much higher; the two brutes were clearly gripped by feeding frenzy. I have called them *Karkomimus* after their horned heads.

Since then, we have seen other species of carnosaur: one foreboding, kingly specimen with tiny arms, one with an elongated snout and coloured frills that was hunting in water, and the most magnificent of all, a huge, head-plated creature with powerful forearms and blood-red scales. All display common features: two thick legs with the toes ending in curved claws, equally thick necks and a large rectangular head tipped with teeth like the spikes on a mace. They are mostly loners, but we also observed that they can hunt in reproductive couples.

They are experienced hunters, able to specialise on different prey. I observed one medium-sized *Carnophaganax* trying to knock down a four-legged reptile with a huge tail ending in a spiked defensive weapon. Its back was armoured and apparently the carnosaur was unable to penetrate it; it tried to overturn its prey, but instead received severe wounds from the tail.

Day 36

We've found a swamp popular with herbivores. The fact they don't see us as a prey doesn't make them less dangerous – many are huge and frequently nervous. We found several new species of thyroscutia, including the tusked *Kentrodon* which had fought off the carnosaur; a turtle-like *Ankylophylus* with impenetrable domed armour and a retractable head; and a family of belligerent beasts which injured one of the trackers with a shower of projectile bone shards. I also had the chance to observe a herd of *Pachykranion* – two legs, small arms, large tail and armored skull cap used as a weapon against predators and other males for social dominion within the herd.

We encountered at least three species of taurosaur, including a bulky, gnarled and ancient-looking *Quintacerasaurus*, and a family of *Styracotops* with dark black scales patterned by glowing colours that only became visible after nightfall. Both are huge, quiet, and slow – I've even touched one, an experience that I will never forget. But once roused, they become unstoppable, with their armoured crest, mighty hooves and unbreakable horns.

2/3

Day 40

May the blessed saints preserve me. We have found the titanopods. These magnificent creatures tower above the trees and other sauria alike, giving a whole new meaning to the word "Magna". Legs like the largest pillars of Avras move barrel-shaped bodies elongated with stupendous tails and necks tipped with a small round head and spoon-shaped teeth to pull leaves from trees. They are slow but immensely sturdy, quiet and gentle, not easily panicked, even by a group of lavishly frilled fire-breathers from the *Salamandria* genus that hunted nearby.

I can only imagine the uses for such beasts in both war and peace should any civilisation be able to tame them. Their size and appearance varies by species; all are gigantic, but we spotted one relatively small *Compsosaurus*, which could change the colours of its scales for camouflage. The biggest were like walking mountains, which is indeed the name the natives give them, *nenemtepetl*: vast, craggy and ancient, with hide that looks more like rugged stone than skin, plants and vines hanging from the crevices and pterosaurs nesting in the crannies.

Among the swooping airborne reptiles, I caught several glimpses of one larger beast bedecked in radiant colours. It appeared to possess the long, coiling body and fangs of an anaconda, but of a larger size and augmented with bright and extravagant plumage. I wonder if I am beginning to hallucinate.

Day 48

We were fools. The captain discovered a nest of titanopod eggs, and despite the warnings of the guides, seized them. We barely made it a day's journey before the remainder of our expedition began to fall to hunters. Not Magna Sauria, this time; there is a cold intelligence pursuing us now. Few of us remain. Still the captain refuses to leave the eggs behind. I do not know if I will ever see my beloved *Poodle* again.

—*Journal of Carlos Daruín, Destrian naturalist*

OTHER ENCLAVES

Oyez, dear public, for today I will reveal tales never heard.

You've heard of saurians, but did you think they were all alike? Giant toads on their flying carts, guarded by agile reptiles riding enormous monsters? That's just the best-known kind of saurians, those which work together around the world. But there are other saurian tribes, more mysterious and more ferocious, despite their lack of Magna Sauria. Those who stick to their own wild customs deep within their hidden lands, rejecting the global union and lacking its values, technologies and pets alike, according to letters I have seen from saurian envoys themselves.

I, Aldulf de Beckdayle, have collected true testimonies, right here in this notebook, directly from the mouths of the most reliable sailors and adventurers to have visited the esteemed Drunken Kraken. Find it facing Ogre's Pier, west bank of the Omiphorus.

Perhaps the closest saurian enclave to our great city is the enemy of the Khasib lords who live west of the Barren Mountains. They say that these saurians dwell in a secret mountain city, Gundê Razdar, with huge granite ramparts and entrances that cannot be found, since they look perfectly like the neighbouring mesas. Some have said that this is an ancient edifice from the Dawn Age – most saurians today try to avoid such remnants, but not these ones. Many a caravan has been lost, not suspecting the danger until it was ambushed by cold-bloods. When (or if) they wake up, the merchants discover their cargo is missing, and they have been moved to a different road altogether. Some say the saurians only take what is edible, and leave precious goods and coins as bait for the next travelers.

Those of you who have sailed out to the Great Ocean have surely glimpsed the Copper Mountains. Here, the nearby oases face sudden raids which seize their crops and strip their palm trees to bare trunks. When they are under attack, the Qassari are terrorised by horrible visions sent by the saurian "god", which is in fact a massive anurarch known as the Troglodyte King. All the saurians are willing to die and to kill for her. They say she escaped long ago from a distant island where she faced execution by Vitalist saurians.

Further south, the potent empire of the Koghi is kept in check at the entrance of the exuberant rainforest. This is the realm of the legendary jungle city of Nsisiboko. It is protected by ferocious tegus riding large cats with dotted fur and powerful fangs, who climb trees and fall on their prey. The caimans wear tusks across their noses; the skinks have large eyes and can change the colour of their scales for camouflage. They venerate the Leopard God, who requires bloody sacrifices. Not only do they hunt all sapient species, humans, elves or halflings, but these cannibals eat them during atrocious ceremonies in front of their gigantic wooden idols. An explorer told me that the only creatures these reptiles fear are the spirits of the jungle themselves, like the implacable Mami Wata which haunts the slow rivers.

The survivors of a Destrian shipwreck, blown onto the Bastion islands, were soon captured and enslaved by a strange tribe of tegus and skinks. These were no warriors, wearing nothing but long, multi-coloured feathers. Instead, all of them were masters of magic, and nothing could be done to resist their occult powers. The crew were stripped of their clothes and forced to live a crude life of service, eating only raw fruits, roots, and seashells. The saurians claimed to be descendants and true defenders of the Dawn Empire; through the endless work of their slaves, they were trying to restore and maintain a sort of ancient, colossal tower. One sailor escaped this hell by jumping on a floating trunk, and was recovered three days later by an Imperial ship.

A one-eyed elf once told me that the worst saurians were to be found south of the Tietha river in his home country. Living deep in the endless swamps, and using alligators, snakes and other poisonous creatures in battle, they could never be surprised, not even by elves. At best, empty huts would be found, with symbolic ochre drawings on the walls. All the expeditions sent against them failed, leaving elven companies lost for months or even years in the marshy labyrinth.

Now, at the opposite edge of the map, in Tsuandan they build massive bamboo ships called junks. With up to seven masts, they are ten times the size of the largest galleons moored in Avras. Despite this, they have encountered something even bigger. A junk was sailing in the high seas when it met a party of saurians, travelling on the back of a ginormous sea turtle the size of a city! The testudine transport came closer to allow the many saurian warmachines to fire. Skinks flying on winged creatures attacked from above, while caimans went under the junk and boarded it from the opposite side. The Tsuandanese fought back; some of the palisades on the turtle's shell took fire from their black powder arsenal. Suddenly, without any signal seen or heard, the saurians turned away and vanished over the horizon.

The most exotic saurian story I have heard may have been told by an ogre visitor with exuberant silk clothes. He had travelled south of the Sky Mountains, where the river Adhika meets the Southern Ocean. Deep in the jungles, there is a nauseating plain, filled with marshes and mud. The dark mangroves and swamps are full of huge snakes, crocodiles, and other predators. The local race of saurians is very distinctive, with albino scales, yellow eyes, and grey teeth. Even stranger is their cult to the Serpent God Shaari, venerated in their inaccessible temple of Lakti Mashetra. From it emerge hordes of Serpent-Warriors, invariably led by the strongest and most violent caiman rulers, carrying heads and trophies of past victims. They subdue local populations, demanding endless adoration of the Avatars of Shaari, as the leaders like to present themselves. Stories claim these saurians once followed the peaceful way of Vitalism, but it seems they gradually twisted and perverted its teachings, becoming perhaps the first enclave to be expelled by the saurian Collaboration. Yet they still believe living things hold power, and so seek to gain that power by consuming the flesh of the living, especially the strongest fighters. The ogre merchant I met was only allowed to leave because he managed to challenge a younger caiman and win barehanded, albeit earning terrible scars in the process.

—Words of a performer in a town square in central Avras

Compatible with
IX AGE
TM
The 9th Age™

THE IX AGE
FANTASY BATTLES

Gather close, ye who would learn of the strange peoples and wondrous places of the Ninth Age. None of us can know the secrets of the entire world, but if you seek a little wisdom on a particular culture or nation, open up this tome and discover what there is to tell.

You seek to learn the lessons of the ancients? The cold-blooded masters of monster and magecraft. Across the world the saurians wait, hidden, looking for the moment to act. Bright eyes in the rocks and bushes. Completely silent... until they are deafening.

www.ingramcontent.com/pod-product-compliance
Lightning Source LLC
LaVergne TN
LVHW060421200726
843506LV00007B/504